Edmund Morse

Wanda

A Drama in Four Acts and Prologue

Edmund Morse

Wanda
A Drama in Four Acts and Prologue

ISBN/EAN: 9783337343156

Printed in Europe, USA, Canada, Australia, Japan

Cover: Foto ©Andreas Hilbeck / pixelio.de

More available books at **www.hansebooks.com**

WANDA.

DRAMA IN FOUR ACTS

AND PROLOGUE.

ADAPTED FROM OUIDA, BY

EDMUND MORSE.

1884.

COURIER COMPANY,
STEAM PRINTERS, EVANSVILLE, INDIANA.

WANDA PROLOGUE.

Paul Zaberoff—
This is pleasant here in this miserable village with a wheel off my telegue! Say, Maro, whose house is that?
Servant—
Master, it is thine!
P. Z.—
Mine! I had forgotten; I suppose my agents know it. Outside of Petersburg, Russia is to me detestable. And here I look around me an absolute stranger in the place where I am absolutely lord. All these square leagues are mine; all these miserable huts; all these poor lives; yet I have a vague remembrance of being here once before.
Servant—
My lord, the vehicle is repaired, and all is ready for our departure.
Maritza—
Stay, my lord! Stay, my lord!
P. Z.—
Who is this?
Blacksmith—
It is only Mad Maritza!
Maritza
Let me come! let me come! I would give him back the jewel he left here ten years ago. All hail to my lord! and heaven be with him. The poor Maritza comes to give him back what he left.
P. Z.—
Nay, good mother, keep it; whatever it be, you have earned the right. Is it a jewel, you say?
Maritza—
It is a jewel.
P. Z.—
Then keep it. I had forgotten that I was ever here.
Maritza—
Aye, the great lord had forgotten? There is the jewel, Paul Ivanovitch! (brings him the child.)

P. Z.—

A handsome child! may the land have many such to serve the Czar. Is he your grandson, good mother?

Maritza—

He is thy son, my lord!

P. Z.—

My son?

Maritza —

Ay! my lord has forgotten; the lord tarried but one night, but he bade my Sacha serve drink to him in his chamber, and on the morrow when he left Sacha wept. The lord has forgotten!

P. Z.—

Where is——the mother?

Maritza—

My Sacha died four summers ago. Always Sacha hoped that the lord might some day return.

P. Z.—

Fool! why did you not marry her? There were plenty of men, I would have given more dowery.

Maritza—

Sacha would not wed, what the lord had honored she thought holy.

P. Z.—

Poor soul! (turning to the boy), do you understand what we say?

Vassia—

I understand.

P. Z.—

What is your name?

Vassia—

Vassia Kazan.

P. Z.—

Are you happy?

Vassia—

What is that? I do not know.

P. Z.—

Rise up, since you are my son!

Maritza—

I have delivered the jewel to the lord who owns it; I have done Sacha's will.

P. Z.—

These jewels are as many as the sands of the sea, and

as worthless! Nevertheless the boy shall be cared for,
and well taught, and have all that gold can get for him;
and be sent away, for here he is only a serf! Farewell!
You are magnificently handsome, my poor child—indeed,
who knows what you will be, a jewel or a toad's eye?
Send him to a great school! send him out of Russia! spare
no cost! make him a gentleman! Again, farewell!

ACT I.

SCENE 1ST.

Wanda—
You cannot carry arms here!
Sabran—
You have lost me the only eagle I have seen for
years.
Wanda—
That bird was not an eagle, sir; it was a white
throated vulture— a Kutengeier; but, had it been an eagle
—or a sparrow—you could not have killed it on my land!
Sabran—
I have not the honor to know in whose presence I
stand. But I have imperial permission to shoot wherever
I choose.
Wanda—
His Majesty has no more loyal subject than myself;
but his dominion does not extend over my forests. You
are on the ground of Hohenszalras, and your offence——
Sabran
I know nothing of Hohenszalras!
Wanda—
You know Hohenszalras now! Men have been shot
dead for what you were doing! If you indeed be a friend
of my Emperor, of course you are welcome here, but——
Sabran
What right have you to do me this indignity?
Wanda
Right! I have the right to do anything with you I
please! You seem to understand but little of forest laws.

Sabran—

Madam, were you not a woman, you would have had bloodshed.

Wanda—

Oh ! very likely. That sometimes happens, although seldom, as all the Hone Tauern know how strictly these forests are preserved. My men are looking to me for permission to break your rifle. That is the law, sir !

Sabran—

Since '48 all the old forest laws are null and void ; it is scarcely allowable to talk of trespass now.

Wanda

The follies of '48 have nothing to do with Hohenszalras. We hold charters of our own by grants and rights, which even Rudolf of Hapsburg never dare meddle with. I am not called upon to explain all this to you, but you appear to labor under such strange delusions that it is well to dispel them. Are you indeed a friend of the Kaiser ?

Sabran—

I am no friend of his; I met him awhile ago, Zad hunting on the Thorstein. His signature is in my pocket ; bid your jagers to take it out.

Wanda

I will not doubt your word. You look a gentleman ; if you will give me your promise to shoot no more on these lands, I will set you free and render you up your rifle.

Sabran—

You have the law with you ; since I can do no less, I promise.

Wanda—

You are ungracious, sir ; that is neither wise nor grateful, since you are nothing more or better than a poacher on my lands. Nevertheless I will trust you. Follow that path into the ravine, cross that, ascend the opposite hills, and you will find the highroad ; I advise you to take it, sir. Good day to you, sir.

Otto—

Alas, my Countess, why have you let him go?

Wanda

The Keiser has made him sacred. What strange creatures we are ! The vulture would have dropped in the ravine ; he would have never found it. The audacity, too, to fire on a Kutengeier! If it had been any lesser bird, one might have pardoned it. Where could the stranger have come from, Otto?

Otto—

He must have come over the Hundspitz, my Countess. Any other way he would have been stopped by our men and lightened of his rifle.

Wanda—

The Hundspitz?——

Otto—

That must be, and for sure, if any honest man had tried to come that way, he would have been hurled head-long down the ice-wall.

Wanda—

He is the Keiser's protege, Otto.

Scene 2d—*Terrace at Hohenszalras.*

Wanda—

How often do we thank God for the mountains? yet we ought every night we pray.

How could I ever forget him, so long as that water glides there. Oh Bela, my dearest brother!

Princess Ottilie—

Yet her majesty is so right—so right, so wise——her majesty is so right.

Wanda—

It would not become my loyal affection to say she could be wrong. But still, I know myself, and I know the world very well, and I for one prefer Hohenszalras to it.

Princess O.—

Hohenszalras is all very well in the summer and autumn, but for a woman of your age and your possessions to pass your days talking to farmers and fishermen, pouring over books, perplexing yourself as to whether it is right for you to accept wealth that comes from such a source of danger to human lives as your salt mines, it is absurd; it is ludicrous. You are made for something more than a political economist; you should be in the great world.

Wanda—

I prefer my liberty and solitude.

Princess O.—

Liberty! Who or what could dictate to you in the world? You reigned there once, you would always reign there.

Wanda—

Social life is a bondage as an Empress's is. It denies one the greatest luxury of life—solitude.

P. O.—

Certainly if you love solitude so much, you have your heart's desire here. It is an Alverina! It is a Mt. Athas! a hermitage only tempered by horses.

Wanda—

By many horses. Certainly dearest Countess, what would you have? Austrians are all centaurs and Amazons. I am only like my Kaiseriun in that passion.

P. O.—

Surely you will go to Ischl or Iodollo this autumn, since her majesty wishes it.

Wanda—

Her majesty is so kind as to wish it. Let us leave time to show what it holds for us. This is scarcely summer; yesterday was the 15th of May.

P. O.—

It is horribly cold; it is always horribly cold here, even in mid summers. And when it does not snow, it rains, you cannot deny *that.*

Wanda—

Come now! we have seen the sun all day to-day; I hope we shall see it many days—they have begun planting out you see. The gardens will soon be gorgeous.

P. O.—

When the mist allows it to be seen, it will be, I dare say. It is tolerable here in the summer, though never agreeable! But the Empress is so right it is absurd to shut yourself up in this gloomy place; you are bound to return to the world. You owe it to your position to be seen in it once more.

Wanda

The world does not want me, my dear aunt, nor do I want the world.

P. O.—

That is sheer perversity——

Wanda—

How am I perverse? I know the world very well, and I know no one is necessary to it unless it be a Herr Von Bismarck.

P. O —

Surely one's own friends and foes—people like one's self in a word must be as interesting as Hans or Peter, Katie or Grethel, with their crampons or their milk pails. Besides there are in the world political movements, in· fluences, interests.

Wanda—

Oh, intrigue? as useful as M'dme de Lamballe's or M'dme de Longuville's? No! I do not believe there is even that in our time, when even diplomacy itself is fast becoming a mere automatic factor in a world that is governed by newspapers, and which has changed the tyrany of wits for the tyrany of crowds. The time has gone by when a coterie of Countesses could change ministries, if they ever did so out of the novels ot Disraeli.

P. O.—

You are very hird to please, I know, but say what you will, it becomes rediculous for a person of your age, your great position and your personal beauty, to immerse yourself e ernally in what is virtually no better than confinement in a fortress.

Wanda—

A court is more of a prison to me. I know both lives, and I prefer this. As for my being hard to please, I think I was very gay and thoughtless before Bela's death. Since then all the earth has grown gray for me.

P. O.—

Forgive me, my beloved!

Wanda—

I understand all you wish for me dear aunt; believe me, I envy people when I hear them laughing light-heartedly among each other. I think I shall never laugh so again.

P. O.—

If you would only marry ——

Wanda—

You think marriage amusing. If you do, it is only because you escaped it.

P. O.—

Amusing! I could speak of no sacrament of our Holy Church as amusing. You rarely display such levity of language. I confess I do not comprehend you. Marriage would give you interests in life which you seem to lack sadly now. It would custom you to the world. It would be a natural step to take with such vast possessions as yours.

Wanda—

It is not likely I shall ever take it.

P. O.—

I know it is not likely; I am sorry that it is not. Yet what nobler creature does God's earth contain than your cousin Egon?　　　　　　　　　　·

Wanda—

Egon? Yes, he is a good and brave and loyal gentleman, none better ; but I shall no more marry him than Donan here will wed the forest doe.

P. O.

Yet he has loved you for more than ten years. But if not he, there are many others—men of high enough place to be above all suspicion of mercenary motives. No woman has been more adored than you, Wanda; look at Hugo Landrassy.

Wanda—

Oh, pray spare me their enumeration. It is like the Catalogue of Ships.

Major Domo—

Would it please the ladies to dine ?

Wanda

What a disagreeable obligation dining is.

P. O.

It is very wicked to think so when a merciful Creator has appointed our appetites for our consolation and support; it is only an ingrate who is not thankful lawfully to indulge them.

Wanda—

That view of them never occured to me. I think you must have stolen it, aunt, from some abbe galant or some chauvinesse as lovely as yourself in the last century. Alas ! if not to care to eat, be ungrateful; I am a sad ingrate. Donan and Neva are more ready subscribers to your creed.

P. O.—
I think we shall have wild weather.
Wanda—
I think so too. It is coming very soon, and I fear
I did a very cruel thing this morning.
P. O.—
What was that?
Wanda—
I sent a stranger to find his way over our hills to Ma-
trey as best he might. He will hardly have reached it by
now, and if a storm should come ——
P. O.—
A stranger?
Wanda—
Only a poacher, but he was a gentleman, which made
his crime the worse.
P. O.—
A gentleman, and you sent him over the hills without
a guide!
Wanda—
Why, he would have shot a Kutengeier!
P. O.—
A Kutengeier is a horrid beast; and a stranger just
for an hour or so, would be welcome.
Wanda—
Even if his name were not in the Hofkalender.
P. O.—
If he had been a peddler or a clockworker, you would
have sent him to rest. For a gentlewoman, Wanda, and
so proud a one as you are, you are curiously cruel to your
own class.
Wanda—
I am always cruel to poachers; and to shoot a vulture
in the month of May!
I am troubled for the traveler; I trust he is safely
housed.
*P. O.—*If he had been a pastry cook from the Engadine,
or a sedicious heretical colporteur from Geneva you would
have sent him into the kitchen to feast.
Wanda—
I hope he is safely housed; it is several hours ago! he
may have reached the post-house.

P. O.—

You have the satisfaction of thinking the Kutengeier is safe setting on some rock tearing a fish to pieces. Will you have some coffee or some tea? You look disturbed my dear. After all you say the man was a poacher.

Wonda—

Yes; but I ought to have seen him safe off my ground. There are a hundred kinds of deaths on the hills for any one who does not know them. Well, let us look at the weather from the hall, we can see better from there.

SCENE 3RD—*The Storm.*

Wanda—

How the mountains echo back the thunder; it sounds like salvoes of artillery. See how redly the beacon of the Holy Vale glimmers through the darkness. The great white peaks and pinnacles flash strangely as the lightning illuminates them. See how gross Wanda in the Glockner towers above all others; in the glow it seems like ice and fire mingled. They are like the great white throne of the Apocalypse. "Open one of those windows and listen. I fancy I heard a shout—a scream—I am not certain; but listen well." Oh Bela, my Bela, think not that I forget.

Hubert—

There is some sound; it comes from the lake. But no boat could live long in that water, my Countess.

Wanda—

No; but we must do what we can. It may be one of the lake fishermen caught in the storm before he could make for home. Ring the alarm-bell, and go out all of you to the water-stairs; I will come too. Make no confusion; there is no danger in the castle; there is some boat, or some swimmer on the lake. Light the terrace beacon, and we shall see. "They may be drowned, I hear nothing. Have you the rope and the life-boat ready? We must wait for more light." "For the love of God, be quick!"

Sabran—

Madam, behold me in your power again.

Wanda—

You are welcome, sir; any stranger or friend would be welcome in such a night. Pray do not waste your

breath or time in courtesies ; come up the steps and hurry
to the house, you must be faint and bruised.

Sabran—

No, no.

Otto—

Keep you still ; you have the Countess' orders. Trespass has cost you dear, my master.

Wanda—

I do not think he is greatly hurt ; but go to him doctor, and see that he is warmly housed, and has hot drinks.
Put him in the stranger's gallery, and pray, take care my
aunt is not alarmed.

Princess Ottilie—

It is unkind of you to go out in that mad way in
such a night as this, and return looking so unlike having
an adventure.

Wanda—

There has been no adventure, but there is what may
do as well. A handsome stranger who has been saved
from drowning. " Bela, my beloved, think not that I forget."

P. O.—

Then there is an adventure; tell me quick ! My
dear, silence is very stately and very becoming to you, but
sometime—excuse me—you do push it to annoying ex-
tremes.

Wanda—

I was afraid of agitating you. The stranger I sent
over the hills was rescued from the lake ; he is unhurt.

P. O.—

And I never knew that a poor soul was in peril, and
is that the last you have seen of him? have you never
asked——

Wanda—

Hubert says he is only bruised. They have taken
him to the stranger's gallery. Here is Herr Greswold !
he will tell us more.

P. O.—

He is a gentleman, think you ?

Greswold.—

Yes.

P. O.—

And of what rank ?

G.—

It is impossible for me to say.

P. O.—

It is always possible. Is his linen fine; is his skin smooth; are his hands white and slender; are his wrists and ankles small ?

G.—

I am sorely grieved, Princess, to say I have taken no notice of these things; I was occupied in my diagnosis of the patient's state; he had been a long time in the water, and the szalresse is of a dangerous temperature at night.

P. O.—

It is very interesting, but pray observe what I have named, now that you return to his chamber. (Exit G.)—— I wish one could know who he is; to harbor an unknown person in these days of democracies and dynamite is not agreeable.

Wanda—

What does it matter; though he were a nihilist or a convict from the mines, he would have to be sheltered to-night. Dear aunt, come with me, I have asked Father Ferdinand to have a mass to-night for Bela. I fancy Bela is glad that no other life has been taken by the lake.

Scene Stranger's Gallery.

Sabran—

Am I in heaven ?

Gresnold—

You are in the burg of Hohenszalras. The music you hear comes from the chapel; there is a midnight mass —a mass of thanksgiving for you.

S.—

Twice in that woman's power. Can I not disentangle the memories from the dreams that haunt me of the Nibelungen queen, who all night long I've seen in her golden armor, with eyes that, like those of the Greek nymph, dazzling them on whom they gaze to madness; has dream and fact so woven themselves I cannot sever the trio ?

G.—

How does the gentleman feel this morning ?

S.—

I saw a lady last night.

G. —

Certainly, you saw our lady.

S. —

What do you call her ?

G. —

She is the Countess Wanda von Szalras; she is sole
mistress here.   But for her, my dear sir, I fear me you
would be now lying in those unfathomed depths, that the
bravest of us fear.

S. —

I was a madman to try the lake with such an overcast
sky, but I missed my road, and I was told that it lay on
the other side of the water; some peasant tried to dis-
suade me from crossing, but I am a good rower and swimmer, too, so I set forth to pull myself over your lake.

G. —

With a sky black as ink ?   I suppose you are used to
more serene summers ; midsummer is not so different from
mid-winter here, that you can trust to its tender mercies.

S. —

She took my gun away from me in the morning; it
makes the bread and wine bitter.

G. —

Were you paoching ?   Oh, that is almost a hanging
offence in the Hohenszalras woods.   Had you met Otto
without our lady he would most likely have shot you without warning.

S. —

Are you savages in the Tauern ?

G. —

Oh, no; but we are very feudal yet, and our forest
laws have escaped alteration in this especial part of the
province.

S. —

She has been very hospitable to me, since my crime
was so great.

G. —

She is the soul of hospitality, and the schloss is a hospice, but take some tokay.   My dear sir you had best lay
still, and I will send you some journals and books.

S. —

I would rather get up and go away.   These bruises
are nothing ; I will thank your lady, as you call her, and

then go on my way as quickly as I can.

G.—

I see you do not understand feudal ways, although you have suffered from them. You may get up if you wish, but I am sure my lady will not let you leave here to-day. The rain is falling in torrents; a bridge has broken down over the Burgenback, which you must cross to get away; if you were to insist they would harness the horses for you, but you would possibly kill the horses, and perhaps the postilions, and then not even get far away; you had far better wait at least until dawn.

S.—

I had rather burden your lady with an unwelcome guest than kill her horses, certainly. How is she sole mistress here? Is there no Count von Szalras; is she a widow?

G.—

She was never married.

S. —

A very happy woman to be so rich and so free; she is very handsome—indeed beautiful. I now remember having heard of her in Paris. Her hand has been esteemed one of the great prizes of Europe.

G.—

I think she will never marry.

S.—

Oh, my dear doctor, who can make such a prophecy for any woman who is still young—at least she looks young; what age may she be?

G.—

She is twenty-four years of age on Ascension Day. As for happiness, when you know the Countess Wanda, you will know that she would go out as poor as St. Elizabeth, and dethroned like her, most willingly, could she by such a sacrifice see her brothers living around her.

S.—

Eh?

G.—

You do not know her.

S.—

I know humanity. You will kindly take all my apologies and regrets to the Countess, and give her my name, the Marquis de Sabran; she can satisfy herself as to my identity, at any embassy she may care to consult.

G.—

Sabran! Sabran!. You! Sabran who edited the "Mexico?"

S.—

Long ago; yes. Have you heard of it?

G.—

Heard of it! Do you take us for barbarians, sir? It is here, both in my small library, which is the collection of a specialist, and in the great library of the castle, which contains half a million of volumes.

S.—

I am twice honored.

G.—

May I not be permitted to congratulate you, sir? To have produced that great work is to possess a title to the gratitude and esteem of all educated men.

S.—

You are very good, but all that is great in that book is the Marquis Xavar's, I am but the mere compiler.

G.—

The compilation, the editing of it required no less learning than the original writer displayed, and that was immense.

S.—

You are very good, but you will forgive me if I say that I have heard so much of the "Mexico" that I am tempted to wish I had never produced it. I did so as a duty; it was all I could do in honor of one whom I owed far more than mere life itself. Give me my belt. Your Countess will doubtless recognize her Emperor's signature; it will serve at least as a passport, if not as a letter of presentation. It is a magnificent hospice; why did she offer me that outrage—to take my rifle from me. It goes hard with me to lie under her roof, to taste her wine and bread. 'Tis trespass on this woman's hospitality. My lad, cannot I get a carriage for Lend? My servant is waiting for me there.

Lad—

There are no carriages here but my lady's, and she will not let you stir this afternoon, my lord.

S.—

But I have no coat.

Lad—

The Herr Professor thought you could perhaps manage with one of these. They are all Count Gela's, who was a tall man and about your make. If you could wear one of these, my lord, for this evening, we will send as soon as it is possible, for your servant and clothes to St. Johann. It is impossible, to-day, because the bridge is down over the Burgenbach.

S.—

You are all of you too good.

What a grand house to be shut up in the heart of the mountains; I do believe what romance there still is in the world, does lie in these forests of Austria, which have all the twilight and the solitude that would suit Merlin or the Sleeping Beauty better than anything we have in France, except, indeed, here and there an old chateau like Chenonceaux or Maintenon.

G.—

The world has not spoiled us as yet; we see few strangers; our people are full of old faiths, old loyalties, old traditions. They are a sturdy and yet a tender people. They are as fearless as their own Steinbock, and they are as reverent as saints, in monastic days. Our mountains are as grand as the Swiss ones; but, thank heaven, they are unspoiled and little known. I tremble when I think of the time—they have begun to climb the Gross Gockner; all the mystery and glory of our glaciers will vanish when they become mere points of ascension. The alpinstock of the tourist is to the everlasting hills what railroad metals are to the plains. Thank God, the few railroads that we have are hundreds of miles asunder.

S.—

You are a reactionist, doctor.

G.—

I am an old man, and I have learned the vale of repose. You know we are called a slow race. It is only the unwise among us who have the quicksilver in their brain and toes.

S.

You have gold in the former, at least, and I dare say quicksilver is in your feet, too, when there is charity to be done.——(Am I not to see her at all?)

G.

This was painted last year, at the Coulit ss' request. It is admirably like her.

S.—

It is a noble picture; but what a very proud woman she looks.

G.—

Blood tells for more than most people know or admit. It is natural; my lady, with the blood of so many mighty nobles in her, should not be proud.

S.—

Where are the ladies?

G.—

The Princess is at her devotions. As for our lady, no one ever pisturbs her or knows what she is doing. When she wants any of us ordinary folks, we are summoned. You know this is an immense estate; a palace at the capitol, and one at Salzberg; not to speak of the large estates in Hungary and the mines of Galecia. All these our lady manages herself; she is her own secretary.

S.—

A second Maria, Theresa.

G.—

Not dissimilar, perhaps. Only where our great queen sent out thousands to their death. The Countess von Szalras saves many lives; there are no mines in the world where there is so much comfort and so little peril as those of her's in Staneslau.

S.—

Heavens how it rains; is that common here?

G.—

Very common; indeed, we pass two-thirds of the year between snow and water; but we have great compensation. Where do you see such graze, such forests, such gardens, where the summer sun does shine?

Hubert—

My lady desires that the Marquis would favor them with his presence! (*Aside*). Look you, since Count Gela rode to his death at the head of the White Hussars, so grand a man as this stranger has not set foot in this house.

ACT II.

P. O —

Monsieur de Marquis, I desire none of your eloquent thanks. Age is sadly selfish; I did nothing to resque you, "unless, indeed, heaven heard my unworthy prayers——" and this house is not mine, nor anything in it. The owner of it is my grand niece, the Countess Wanda von Szalras.

S. —

That I had your intercessions with prayer, however indirectly, is more than I deserve. For the Countess Wanda, I have been twice in her power, and she has been very generous.

P. O. —

She has done her duty, nothing more; as for leaving us this day, it is out of the question. The storm is terrible! I fear it is even impossible for your servant to come from St. Johann.

S. —

I have wanted for nothing, and my Parisian rogue is quite as well gaming and smoking his days away at Sanct Johann. How can I ever express all my sense of profound obligations to you who have laid me under, stranger that I am.

P. O. —

At least we were bound to atone for the incivility of the Szalrasse. It is a very horrible country to live in; my niece thinks it Arcadia. But an Arcadia subject to the most terrible floods and frosts and snows, does not commend itself to me; no doubt it is very grand and romantic ——(can he be some crown prince in disguise ? no, I know every crown prince in Europe). My niece, the Countess Wanda, begs you to excuse her, she is tired from the storm last night.

S.—Aside.

(She does not wish to see me). You leave me nothing to regreat Princess.

P. O.—Aside.

(I have said she was tired, she who is never more tired than the eagles are). You have no appetite ?

S. —

Pardon me, I have a good one, but I have always been content to eat little and drink less; it is the secret of health, and my health is all my riches.

P. O.—

I should think your riches in that respect inexhaustible.

S.—

Oh, yes; I have never had a day's illlness, except once long ago in the Mexican swamps.

P. O.—

You have traveled much.

———

P. O.—

It is my niece, the Countess Von Szalras——Wanda, my love, I was not aware you were here; I thought you were in your own room. Allow me to make you acquainted with your guest, whom you have already received twice with little ceremony I believe.

Wanda—

I fear I have been inhospitable, sir; are you wholly unhurt? You had a rough greeting from Hohenszalras.

S.—

I am but a vagrant, madam; and have no right even to your charity.

Wanda—

You were a poacher, certainly, but that is forgiven. My aunt has taken you under her protection; you had the Keiser's already. With such a dual shelter you are safe; are you quite recovered? I have to ask your pardon for not sending one of my men to guide you to Matrey.

S.—

Nay, if you had done so, I should not have enjoyed the happiness of being your debtor. You——

Wanda—

Pray carry no such burden of imaginary debt, and have no scruples in staying as long as you like; we are a mountain refuge, use it as you would a monastery. But how came you on the lake last evening; can you not read the skies?

S.—

I am a strong swimmer and a good rower; I had no fear and thought to cross before the storm broke The offending rifle is in the Szalrasse. It was my haste to quit your dominion that made me venture on the lake.

Wanda—

No, for many leagues you would not have been off it

P. O.—

"All is well that ends well!" Monsieur is not the worse for his bath in the lake, and we have the novelty of an incident and of a guest who we will hope in the future will become a friend.

S.—

Madam, if I dare hope, I had so much to live for.

P. O.—

You must have very much to live for as it is. Were I a man as young as you, and as favored by nature, I should be tempted to live for myself.

S.—

And I am most glad to escape from so poor a companion.

I have trespassed too long on your patience, madam ; I have the honor to wish you good night.

Wanda—

If there be a Lorelei in our lake no wonder she tried to drown you. Good night, sir; should you wish to leave us in the morning, Hubert will see you reach Sanct Johann safely and quickly as can be.

S.—

Your goodness overwhelms me ; I can never hope to show my gratitnde.

Wanda—

There is nothing to be grateful for. Good night, sir, may you have a good rest and a fair journey. It is actually twelve. (Exit S.)

P. O.—

Acknowledge at least he has made the evening pass well.

Wanda—

He has made it pass admirably; at the same time dear aunt I think it would have been perhaps better if you had not made a friend of a stranger.

P. O.

Why ?

Wanda—

Because I think we can fulfill all the duties of hospitality without doing so, and we know nothing of the stranger—

P. O.

He is certainly a gentleman——it seems to me, my dear Wanda, that you are for once in your life—pardon me—ill-natured.

Wanda

I cannot imagine myself ill-natured, but I may be so; one never knows one's self.

P. O.

And ungrateful, when I should like to know have you for years reached twelve o'clock at night without being concious of it.

Wanda

Oh, he read superbly. But let him go on his way to-morrow; you and I cannot entertain strange men, even they put so much soul in Goethe.

P. O.—

If Egon were here.

Wanda—

Oh, poor Egon! I think he would not like your friend at all. They both want to shoot eagles.

P. O.—

Perhaps he would not like him for another reason; Egon could never read Goethe.

Wanda

No! but—who knows! perhaps he can take better care of his own soul, because he cannot lend one to poetry.

P. O.—

You are perverse, Wanda.

Wanda—

Perverse, inhospitable and ill-natured. I fear I shall have a heavy burden of sins to carry to Father Ferdinand in the morning.

P. O.—

I wish you would not send horses to St. Johann in the morning.

ACT III.

Scene 1st.

Wanda—

Why do you avoid me? My men sought you in all directions. I wish to thank you.

Sabran--

I ventured to be near at hand to be of use to you. I was afraid the exposure, the damp, and all this pestilence would make you ill.

Wanda—

No; I am quite well. I have heard of all your courage and endurance. Idrac owes you a great debt.

S.—

I only pay my debt to Hohenszalras.

Wanda—

How did you know of the innundation? It was unkind of you not to come to me.

S.—

You are too good; thousands of men much better than I suffered much more.

Wanda—

You have much to tell me, and I much to hear; you should have come to the monastery to be cured of your wounds; why are you so mistrustful of our friendship. Indeed, we can honor brave men in the Tauern and in Idrac, too. You are very brave; I do not know how to thank you for myself or my people.

S.—

Pray do not speak so; to see you again would be recompense, for much worthier things than any I have done.

Wanda—

But you might have seen me long ago, had you chosen to come to the Isle. I asked you twice.

S.

Do not tempt me. If I yielded, and if you despised me——

Wanda—

How could I despise one who so nobly saved the lives of my people?

S.—

You would do so. One evening, when we spoke together on the terrace, you leaned your hand upon the ivy there. I plucked the leaf you touched; you did not see me. I had the leaf with me all through the war; it was a talisman; it was like a holy thing. When your cousin soldiers stripped me in their ambulance, they took it from me.

IVanda—

I have much to thank you for. (*Aside*---After all, if we love each other, what is it to any one else; we are both free). My friend, did never you think that out? I also——They robbed you of your ivy leaf, my cruel Prussian cousins. Will you --t1ke---this---instead.

S.—

Oh, my beloved! is this heaven itself opened to my eyes?

P. O.—

My dear, is it indeed so? you were very wise to listen to your heart.

Wanda—

Perhaps after all it is the wisest to be unwise.

P. O.—

God speaks it; I shall be content to know that when our Father calls me, I will not leave you alone; it is well to have human love close to us.

Wanda—

It is to lean on a reed, perhaps, and when the reed breaks, though it has been so weak before it becomes of iron, barbed and poisoned.

P. O.—

What gloomy thoughts! and you have made me so happy. Surely you are happy yourself?

Wanda—

Yes; my reed is in full flower, but——but——yes, I am happy; I hope that Bela knows.

P. O.—

Ah! he loves you so well.

Wanda—

That I am sure of, yet I might never have known it but for you.

P. O.—

I did it for the best; I have been his frend always; You cannot say so much Wanda, you were very harsh.

Wanda—

Yes, I know; I will atone to him.

P. O.—

And she will make her atonement generously! grandly! She may have to bear pains, griefs, infidelities, calamities; she would otherwise have escaped, bul even so, how much bettter the summer day even with the summer storm

than the dull, grey, quiet windless weather.
Kalnitz—

This is no marriage for her.
P. O.—

Why not; it is a very old family.
K.—

But quite decayed; long ruined.   This man himself
was born in exile.
P. O.—

As they exile everybody twice in every ten years in
France——
K.—

And there have been stories——
P. O.—

Of whom are there no stories?   Calumny is the par-
asite of character; the stronger the character, the closer
to it clings the strangler.
K.—

I never heard him accused of any strength, except of
the wrist in fencing.
P. O.—

Do you know anything dishonorable of him; if you
do you are bound to say it?
K.—

Dishonorable is a grave word. No, I cannot say that
I do; the society he frequents is a guarantee against that,
but his life has been indifferent, complicated, uncertain;
not a life to be allied with that of such a woman as
War.da.   My dear Princess, it has been a life *Dans le
Milieu Parisien ;* what more would you have me say ?
P. O.—

Prince Archambaud's has been that; yet three years
since you earnestly pressed his suit on Wanda.
K.—

Archambaud ? He is one of the first alliances in
Europe ; he is of royal blood, and he has not been more
vicious than other men.
P. O.—

It would be better had he been less so, since he lives
so near the fierce light that beats upon the throne-- an
electric light that blackens while it illumes.   My good
Kaulnitz, you wonder very far afield, if you know any-

thing serious against M. de Sabran, it is your duty to
say it.

K.—

He is hardly more than an adventurer.

P. O.—

He counts his ancestry in unbroken succession, from
the day of Dagobert.

K.—

He has nothing but a league or two of rocks and sand
in Brittany. Yet, though so poor, he made money enough
by cards and speculation to be three years the *Amant en
titre of Cochonette.*

P. O.—

I think we will say no more, my dear baron. The
matter is not your's or mine to decide; Wanda will surely
do as she likes.

K.—

But you have great influence with her.

P. O.—

I have none; no one has any; and I think you do
not understand her in the least; It may cost her very
much to avow to him that she loves him; but, once having done that, it will cost her nothing at all to avow it to
the world; she is much too proud a woman to care for the
world.

Lilienhohe—

He is *gentilhomme de race,* I grant.

P. O.—

When has a noble of Brittany been otherwise?

L.—

I know, but you will admit that he occupies a different position—an invidious one.

P. O. —

And he carries himself well, tho' it is a different position, which is the test of breeding, and I deny entirely that
it is what you call an invidious one; it is you who have the
idea of the crowd when you lay so much stress on the
mere absence of money.

L.—

It is the idea of the crowd that dominates in this age.

P. O. —

The reason for us to resist it if it be so.

L.—
I think you are in love with him yourself, sister mine.
P. O.—
I should be were I forty years younger.
Wanda—
Since I am convinced of the honesty and purity of his motives, what matters the opinion of others.
P. O.—
How can he tell that the world may not some day induce you to doubt these motives.
Wanda—
But he will cease to think of any disparity when all that is mine has been his a year or two. All the people shall look upon him as their lord, since he will be mine, even if I think differently from him on any matter. I will not say it, lest I should remind him that the power lies with me; he shall be no prince consort, he shall be king. I shall abandon to him Idrac; he will be grand Sejneur of Idrac, and I shall be glad for him to bear an Austrian name.
P. O.—
My dear, be cautious, your horses even though you know them, may show you the dangers of too loose rein.
Wanda—
I want no rein at all; you forget to my thinking, marriage should never be a bondage. If one must yield it must be the woman.
P. O.—
These are very fine theories.
Wanda—
I hope to put them in practice. To what I love best on earth shall I dole out a niggard longesse from my wealth. If I were capable of doing so, he would in time grow to hate me, and his hatred would be justified.
P. O.—
I never would have supposed you would become so romantic.
Prince L.—
It will make him independent of you.
Wanda—
That is what beyond all I desire him to be.

Cardinal V.—Aside.

(It is ah infatuation, when Prince Egon, her cousin, would have brought to her a fortune as large as her own.

P. O.—

You think water should always run to the sea ; surely there is a great waste sometimes.

C. V.—

I think you are as infatuated as she ; you forget had she not been inspired with this unhappy sentiment she would most probably left Hohenszalras to the church.

P. O.—

She would have done nothing of the kind. Your eminence mistakes Hohenszalras and everything else ; had'she died unmarried would have gone to the Hapsburgs.

C. V.—

That would have been better than to an adventurer——

P. O.—

How can you call a Breton Noble an adventurer ? it is one of the purest arristocracies of the world if poor.

C. V.—

It is not the first time the church has been worsted by a woman.

Wanda—Asid.

(So will he be always his own master. What pleasure that your kawk stays by you, if you chain him to your wrist ? if he loves you he will sail back uncalled from the longest flight. I think mine always will ; if not---if not--- well, he must go.) My darling, I want you to promise me one thing——

S.—

I promise you all things ; what is this one ?

Wanda—

It is this : You are troubled at the thought that I have one of those great fortunes which form the *acte d' accusation* of socialists against society, and that you have lost all but the rocks and salt beach of Romanis Now, I want you to promise me never to think of this fact ; it is beneath you ! Fortune is so precarious a thing, so easily destroyed by war or revolution, that it is not worth contemplation as a serious barrier between human beings. A treachery, a sin, even a lie--- any one of these may be a wall of adamant, but a mere fortune ! promise me you will never think of mine, except inasmuch, my beloved, as it may inhance my happiness by ministering to yours; look, I had the lawyers bring this over for you to see. It is the deed by which Steven, first Christian King of Hungary, confirmed to the Counts of Idrac in the year 1001 all their fudal rights.

Sabran—

What have I to do with Idrac?

Wanda—

My love can do just as I want with Idrac; you must take it all—the town and the title, and all they bring; it will become you so well, the Count von Idrac. Rise, Count von Idrac!

S.—

On this rose I swear my fealty now and forever. *Aside.* (Would to heaven I had had no other wants than this one you gave me; would that I could forget that ever I lived before—forget that all my life I am unworthy of you). My love, let me live only from the day that will make me your vassal and your——

Wanda—

That will make you my lord. (Kisses him.)

My love, you seem to have forgotten Romanis; I am glad you love the Tauern so, but let us go and see Romanis.

S.—

Romanis! I hate its name—I was very wretched there. I tried to take interest in it because you bade me, but 1 failed; all I saw, all I thought of, was yourself, and I believed you as far and forever removed from me as though you dwelt in some other planet. No, perhaps I am superstitious; I do not wish you to go to Romanis, I believe it would bring us misfortune: the sea is full of treachery, the sands are full of graves.

Wanda—

Superstition is a sort of parody of faith; I am sure you are not superstitious? I do not care to go to Romanis; I like to cheat myself into the belief you were born and bred here. Otto said to me the other day, "My lord must be a son of the soil or how could he know our mountains so well as he does, and how could he anywhere have learned to shoot like that."

S.—

I am glad Otto does me so much honor; when he first met me he would have shot me like a fox if you had given him the word. Ah, my love, how often I think of you that day; you were truly a chatelain of the old mystical German days. You had some mountain flowers in your hand; they were the key flower to my soul, though, alas! I fear you found no treasures on your entrance there.

Wanda—

I will not answer you, since it wonld be flattery to you. By the way, when shall we invite to meet the Grand Duke Lilienhohe; will you make out a list?

S.—

The Grand Duke does not share Princess Ottilie's goodness for me.

Wanda—

What would you! he has been made of buckram and parchment! besides which anything that is not German has --to his mind--no right to exist. By the way, Egon wrote to me this morning he will be here at last.

S.

Your cousin Egon! Here?

Wanda—

Why are you so surprised? I was sure that sooner or later he would conquer that feeling of being unable to meet you. I begged him to come now; it is eight whole years since I have seen him; when once you have met him you will be friends——for my sake.

S.—

Why, do you suppose it would be any easier for him now than then? Men who love you do not change; the meeting can but be painful to Prince Vasarhely.

Wanda—

Dearest, my nearest male relative and I cannot go on forever without seeing each other. Even these years have done Egon a great deal of harm. He has been absent from court for fear of meeting us, and confined himself to his estates until he has grown morose and solitary. I do not wish to have the remorse upon me of having caused the ruin of his gallant and brilliant life. When he is once here he will like you; brave men, have always a certain sympathy. When he has seen you here he will realize that destiny is unchangable and grow reconciled to the knowledge that I am your wife.

S.—alone.

(The thought of that man troubles and alarms me; I dre d my first meeting with that maygar prince prince, and as years have dropped by one after another, and he has fail d to find courage to see us. I h d hoped we would forever remain strangers, but he will now be our guest; and we have been so happy, and now on our cloudless heaven there seems to rise a cloud no larger than a man's hand, but bearing with it disaster and a moonless night. Perhaps he might have forgotten we were so young then; he was not even as old as I. God save her from suffering by me.

SCENE 2D.

Wanda—

Come dear, Egon has arrived; come and welcome him.

S.—

Receive your cousin first alone. He must resent my presence here; I will not force it on him, on the threshold of your house.

Wanda—

Of *our* house; why do you use the wrong pronoun? Believe me, dear, Egon is too generous to bear you the animosity you think.

S.—

Then he never loved you. Well, I will come if you wish it, but I think it is not in the best taste to so assert myself.

Wanda—

Egon is only my cousin and your guest. You are the master of Hohenszalras. Come, it was not so difficult when you received the Emperor.

S.—

I had done the Emperor no wrong.

Wanda—

You have done Egon none; I should not have been his wife had I never been your's.

S.—

Who knows? (*Advances to meet Egon*). My wife has bidden me welcome you Prince Vasarheley, but it would be presumption in me, a stranger, to do that. All her kindred must be dear and sacred here.

Vasarhely—

I am pleased to know yon hold with such esteem our relationship. The Thauern is indeed very dear to me, Wanda; I am pleased to see you well and——happy.

Wanda—

Egon, this is my Bela; you will love him for my sake.

V.—

May the spirit of your lost Bela be with him and dwell in his heart; better I cannot wish him. (*To Sabran* ---Your son is a noble child; you may have reason to be proud of him; he is very like you in feature; I see no trace of the Szatras.)

S.—

The other boy is more like Wanda. As for my daughter, she is too young for any one to say whom she will resemble. All I desire is that she should be like her mother, physically and spiritually.

V.—

True---and what do you like best to do, my little one?

Bela—

To ride.

V.—

There you are a true Szalras, at least. And your brother Gela, can he ride yet? Where is Gela, by the way?

B.—

He is asleep---he's a little thing. Yes, he rides, but it is a chair saddle, it is not real riding.

P.—

I see! Well, when you come and see me, you shall have some real riding on wild horses. On the great steppes of Tartary there are great herds of young wild horses, and some day we will have a great ride.

B.—

Bela will come to Hungary; I think I have great lands there; Otto said so.

S.

Bela has nothing at all. He talks nonesense sometimes, and he had better go sleep with his brother.

V.

I suppose Gela will take your title?

S.

They are babies; it will be time enough when they are court pages or cadets to settle these matter. They are Gela and Bela at present. The only real republic is childhood.

Wanda

I am afraid Bela is the Tyrannus to which all republics secumb. He is extensively autocratic in his notions, in all his make-believe games he is crowned.

V.

He is a beautiful child.

Wanda

Oh, yes! he is so like Rene.

V. Aside.

(Where have I seen those blue eyes, those level brows, those delicate curved lips? They are so familiar, yet so strange to me. When I would name them they seem to recede back in the shadows of some far away past, so far I cannot recall them.)

SCENE 3D.

Baron K.

What do you think of Sabran?

V.

He is a perfect gentleman, a charming companion, and plays admirably at *E'carte*.

B. K.

E'carte, I spoke of his moral worth; what is your impression of that?

V.

If he had not satisfied her as to that, Wanda would not be his wife. He has given her beautiful children, and it seems to me he renders her perfectly happy; we should all be grateful to him.

B. K.

The children are certainly very beautiful.

V.

The people all around are deeply attached to him, and the attachment is genuine. The men of the old archduchy are not easily won; it is only qualities of daring and manliness that appeal to their sympathies.

V.—

I conclude you knew the Marquis de Sabran well in France.

K.—

No, I cannot say that I did; I knew him by repute; that was not very pure. However, the Fauburg always received and entertained him ; the Count de Chambord did the same—they were the most interested. One cannot presume to think they could be deceived.

V.—

Deceived! that is a singular word to use. Do you mean to imply the possibility of any falsity on his part— any intrigue to appear what he is not?

K

No! honestly I cannot say so much. An impression was given me at the moment of his signing his marriage contract that he concealed something, but it was a mere suspicion. All his papers were of unimpeachable regularity. There were never a doubt hinted by anyone, and yet I will confess to you, my dear Egon, since we are speaking in confidence, that I have always had my own doubts as to his Marquisate of Sabran.

V.—

Great God! why do you not stop the marriage?

B. K.—

One does not stop a marriage by a mere baseless suspicion; I have not one shadow of reason for my conjecture ; It merely came into my head at the signing of the contract. I had done all I could to oppose the marriage, but Wanda was inflexible, besides few men are more attractive than Sabran, and as he is one of us, whatever else he be his honor is now our honor.

V.—

One could always kill him and set here free if one were sure.

K.—

You maygar gentlemen always think that every knot can be cut by the sword. If he were a mere adventurer, which is hardly the possible, it would not mend matters by running him through the heart; there are his children.

V.—

Would the marriage be legal if his name were assumed ?

K.—

Oh, no ; she could have it annulled of course, both by church and law ; all those pretty chidlren would have no rights or no name. But we are talking in a very wild and theatrical fashion.   He is as certainly Marquis de Sabran as I am Karl von Kautnitz.

O.—

It is really the knights love for his lady.

S.—

Yes; and I think, countess, that if there were more like my lady on earth, knighthood might revive on other scenes than Wagner's.   (To Wanda.)—She is a cruel and perilous woman.

Wanda—

No, love, she has always seemed to me a mere fashionable and frivolous woman, like so many others of her world.

S.

No, you are wrong.   She is not a butterfly; she has too much energy; she is a profoundly immoral woman also.   Look at her eyes.

Wanda—

That is Stefans affair not ours.   He is indifferent.

S.—

Or unsuspicious.   Did your brother care for her?

Wanda—

He was madly in love with her.   She was only sixteen when he married her.   He fell at Soleferino half a year later.   Then she married my cousin Stefan.   It both shocked and disgusted me.   Perhaps I was foolish to take it thus, but it seemed such a sin against Gela.   To die so and not to be even remembered.

S.—

Did your cousin approve this second marriage?

Wanda—

No; he opposed it.   He had our feeling about it. But Stefan was young and beyound control.   He had the fortune and the title of his mother, the Countess Brancka, and Olga bewitched him as she had done my brother.

S.—

She is a witch, a wicked witch.

O. —*Aside.*

(Can't I make these two men enemies; a duel or an affair of some sort to amuse me.)   M. Sabran, do you know when Egon is to leave?   By the way, you cannot expect him to love you any too well.   You know he was the betrothed of Wanda from her childhood.

S. —

I was quite aware of that before my marriage, but those family arrangements are tranquil disposals of destiny, which if disturbed leave no great, trace of trouble. The prince is still young, and has no lack of consolation, if he needs it, and I cannot believe that he does.

O. B. —

You know as well as I that Egon adores the very stirrup your wife's foot touches.

S. —

I know he is her much beloved cousin.

O. B. —

So you are proof. Well I hope you will prove worthy of my capture. Now for the other. Dear Egon, why did you not stay on the steppes or remain with your Hussars. You make Sabran jealous.

V. —

Jealous! He has much cause when she has neither eye nor ear, neither memory or thought of any kind for any living thing except himself and those children who are his portraits. Why do you say these follies, Olga? You know Wanda chose from all the world, and loves him as no one would suppose she could love mortal.

O. B. —

What do you think of him?

V. —

Every one asks me that question. I am not his keeper.

O. B.

But you must form some opinion. He is virtually Lord of Hohenzalras, and I believe she has made over to him all of Idrac, and his children will have everything.

V. —

Are they not her natural heirs? Who should inherit from her if not her sons?

O. B. —

Of course. Bnt they will inherit nothing from him. It was certainly a great stroke of fortune for a landless gentleman like him. Why is it a certain class of poor gentlemen always captivate noble women?

V. —

What do you mean to insinuate, Ogla Brancka?

O. B.—

Oh nothing, only his history is peculiar. I remember his arrival in France; his first appearonce in society. It is many years ago now. All the Fauberg received him, but some said at the time it was too romantic to be true. Those Mexican forests, that long exile of the Sabran, the sudden appearance of this beautiful young marquis; you will grant it was romantic. I suppose it was the romance that made even Wanda's dear head turn a little. And then such a life in Paris after it—duels, baccarra sudden fortunes, clever comedies, a touch like Liszts, a sudden success in the Chamber, it was all so romantic. It was bound to bring him at last to his haven. The Prince Charmant of an enchanted castle, only enchanted castles sometimes grow dull, and Prince Charmants are not always answerable by tne same Chatelaine.

V.—

Look here, Olga, I am not sure what you mean, but I believe you are tired of seeing my cousins happiness, merely because it is something with which you cannot interfere. For myself, I would protect her happiness as I would her honor if I thought either endangered. Whether you or I like the Marquis de Sabran is beyond the question. She loves him, and she has made him one of us. His honor is now ours. For myself, I would defend him in his absence as though he were my own brother. Not for his sake at all, but for hers. I do not express myself very well, but you know what I mean. Here is Max returning to claim you; now beware how you act.

SCENE 4TH.

Nurse—

Ah, my lord, the little Count is like the Marquis, and so is Herr Gela. You remember, my lord, the noble gentlemen whose names they bear? God send they may be like them in their lives and not in their deaths.

V.—

An early death is good.

Nurse—

Count Bala is not like our saint who died. He is always masterful and loves his own way. My lady is strict with him, and wisely so; for he is a proud and rebelious child. But he is very generous and has noble ways. Count Gela is a little angel; he will be like the dead ones.

V.—

My God! He is like Vassia Kazan. That is, ihe face. That has forever evaded my remembrance. Here, woman!

Nurse—

Poor, gallant gentleman. He wishes these pretty boys were his. Well, it might have been better had he been master here, though there is nothing against the one who is so. Still a stranger is always a stranger, and foreign blood is bad.

V.

Sabran, one moment. Twenty years ago I, a little lad, accompanied my father on a summer visit to the house of a Russian prince, Paul Zabaroff. It was a house gay, magnificent, full of idle men and women of facile charms. Not a house for youth; but both my father and Prince Zabaroff were men of easy morals. At that house was present a youth some years older than I; his name was Vassia Kazan; he had wit and beauty, skill in games and daring in sport. It was understood, without ever being openly said, that he was a natural son of Prince Zabaroff I had knowledge enough of life to know he was base born, and my natural pity I could but curb with contempt; yet my natural intelligence was no match for his subtle and cultured brain. One day one of the lovely ladies there amused herself with a war of words between us. He so exasperated me with his satyrs I flung this taunt in his face, "Were you in Russia you would be a serf." Without a word he sprang upon me, and with a grasp of steel thrashed me with his whip. That from one who, to me, was a slave and a hound, was more than I could bear. I snatched from the table near a dagger and plunged it in his shoulder. Am I mad or is it true? Let me see your shoulder. Have you the mark of the wound I gave you? Your little child has the face of Vassia Kazan. Are you Vassia Kazan? Are you the bastard of Paul Zabaroff? Are you the wolf the steppes? He has swooned you see. I commit him to your hands. I am not needed.

SCENE 5TH.

V.—

Who is there ? Is there anything wrong ?

S.—

It is I; open. You know who I am.

V.—

Yes.

S.—

How did you know it?

V.—

I remembered.

S.—

Will you tell her ?

V.—

I will never tell her.

S.—

You will not ? But you loved her ?

V.—

If I loved her, what is that to you? It is perhaps because I loved her that your foul secret is safe with me now. I shall not tell her. I waited to say this to you. I could not write it lest it should meet her eyes. You came to ask me this ? Be satisfied and go.

S.—

I came to ask you this because had you said otherwise I would have shot myself ere she would have heard.

V.—Aside.

Suicide, the Sclav's courage and serf's refuge.

S.—

I do not thank you. I understand you. Spare me for her sake, not mine.

V.—

Go; you have got my word. Though we lived fifty years you are safe from me, because, God forgive you, you are hers.

O. B.—

What meant that midnight visit ? And who is Vassia Kazan ? That I must know. It is some secret between them. The name is Russian. I shall write to my cousin, who is a member of the third section at St. Petersburg; they who know everything, the past, present and future of everybody.

O. B.—

How very handsome they are; they are just like Sabran. And yet they are not at all a Russian type.

W.—

Why should they be Russian? We have no Russian blood.

Scene 6th.

O. B.—

I do not know what I was thinking of. Sabran always reminds me of my old friend Paul Zabaroff. They are very alike.

W.—

I have seen the present Prince Zabaroff. He is not as I remember him, much like M. de Sabran.

O. B.—

Oh, of course he is not equal to your Apollo. Do you and Rene absolutely never quarrel?

W.—

Quarrel! My dear Olga, how very bourgeois you speak.

O. B.

Do you suppose only the bourgeois quarrel! Really you live in your enchanted forest until you forget what the world is like. It is a cruel thing there is not one divorce law for all the world. If Stefan and I could only set each other free, we should have done it years and years ago.

W.

I did not know your griefs against Stefan was so great.

O.—

Oh! I have no great griefs against him, but we are both bankrupt, and we don't know why, but we both detest each other.

S.—

Madam Brancka, you affected not to understand a message I sent you by Greswold. You will not misunderstand me now when I repeat that you must leave the house of my wife before another night.

O.—

Ah! I am to leave the house of your wife, my cousin, who was once my sister-in-law? And will you tell me why?

S.—

You have a short memory, I believe, Countess; at least your lovers have said so in Paris. But I trust you can spare me the coarseness and brutality of further explanation.

O.—

Ah! How scrupulous you are about trifles. Why not about great things? What does the holy writ tell us? One strains at a gnat and swallows a camel. I once heard a professor say that the translation was not correct, but——

S.—

Pardon me, madam; but I can have no trifling.

O.—

Ah! And if I do not choose to comply with your desire, how do you intend to enforce it?

S.

That is my affair.

O.—

You will make a scene with my husband that will be useless and theatrical. Sefan is one of those men who are always swearing at their wives in private, but in public never admit otherwise than they are otherwise than saints.

S.—

Pardon me, I have no time to listen to your experiences. The Couetess Szalras is aware I came to see you, and I tell you frankly I will not stay more than ten minutes in your rooms.

O.—

You have told her?

S.—

I would have told her all, how you have tried to betray her confidence, but she stopped me with my words unspoken. What think you she said—said of you, the vilest enemy—the only enemy she has!—that if you had graver faults than she knew, she wished not to hear them; you were her relative, and once had been her brother's wife.

O.—

Poor Wanda! She was always so heroic.

S.—

Madam Brancka, this conversation if of no use; you must leave Hohenszalras in the next few hours.

O. —

Wait a moment ; are you judicious in making me an enemy ?

S. —

I much prefer you as an enemy. As a friend you are perilous. I have thehonor to wish you farewell.

S. —

Tell me one thing before you go. Does Wanda know that you are Vassia Kazan ? You have not answered my question. Does Wanda know it ? Does such a saintly woman compound a felony ? I believe a false name is a sort of felony, is it not ? It was an ingenious device, but it was scarcely wise. Things are always found out sometime or another ; at least, m 'n's secrets are. A woman can keep hers. It is very strange that Wanda, of all people, should have made such a misalliance and had such an imposture passed off on her. I belong to her family ; I ought to abhor you, and yet I can imagine your temptation if I cannot forgive it. Still it was a foolish thing to do, not worthy a man of your wit, and in France I believe the punishment for such an assumption is some years imprisment. And here, perhaps you know your marriage would be null and void if she chose.

S —

Hold your peace ! Speak truth if you can. What has Vasarhely told you ?

O —

All !

S —

And he gave me his word.

O —

His word to you when he is in love with your wife ? The miracle is that he has not told her. She would divorce you, and after a decent interval I dare say she would marry him, if only for revenge. For a man so devoted to her as you are, you have certainly contrived to outrage and injure her in the most complete manner. My dear Marquis, to think how fooled we were all the time by you. You so haughty, so fastidious, so patrician. But why are you so dejected ? You know—you know—I was willing ever to be your friend. I am not less willing now. When we last met you offended, you outraged me. Only few moments ago you insulted me as though I were the lowest

creature on the Paris Asphalte. Yet all this I—I—should
be tempted to forgive if you love me as I believe that you
do. I love you, not as that cold, calm, unerring woman
yonder may, but as those only can who know and care for
no heaven but earth. Rene—Vassia—who knowing your
sin, your shame, your birth, your treachery, would say to
you what I say. Not Wanda. Listen, I love you, I love
you. I care nothing what you were borne, what sins you
have sinned, I love you. Love me and she shall never
know. I will silence Egon, I will bury your secret as
though it were one that would cost me my life if it were
known.

S.—

You are even viler than I thought. How long would
you spare me if I sinned against her with you. Go, do
your worst, say your worst. But if you stay beneath my
wife's roof, to-night I will drive you out of the house before all her people, if it be the last act of my authority in
Hohnszalras.

O.—

I love you.

S.—

How dare you speak of love to me? You force me
to use the language of the gutter. If Egon Vasarhely has
put me in your power, use it like the incarnate fiend you
are. I ask no mercy of you, but if you dare to speak of
love to me I will strangle you where you stand. Since you
call me the wolf of the steppes, you shall feel my fangs.

O.—

(Reads.) "Loved Wanda, will you be so good as to
come to me for a moment at once?" Take this to my
cousin, the countess, yourself and report to me. He will
kill himself if he does not strangle me, and so will escape.
Pshaw, we are people of the world; society is with us even
in our solitude. These violent crimes are not ours. We
strike otherwise than with our hands.

Page—

My lord, a message.

S.—

(Reads.) "Olga asks me to come to her. Do you
wish me to do so?" Oh most faithful of all friends. Where
is the countess?

Page—

In the library, my lord.

S.—

Say that I will be with her there in a few moments. You dared to send for her, then?

O.—

Dared? Is that a word to be used by a Russian Moujik as you are to me, the daughter of Fedor Demetrivitch Serriatine? Certainly I sent for wife, my cousin, who should know what I know if not she. Egon might make you what promises he would. He is a man and a fool! I make none. You may prevent me seeing Wanda. I shall write to her. If you stop her letters I shall telegraph to to her. If that fails, then I will put your story in the Paris journals, where the Marquis de Sabran is as well known as the Arc de l'Etoile. You were born a serf; you shall feel the knout. It would have been well for you if you had smarted under it in your youth.

S.—

Spare your threats; no one will tell her but myself. You know her present condition; it will most likely kill her.

O.—

Oh no, her nerves are of iron; she will divorce you, that is all.

S.—

She will be in her right.

O.—

For a bastard he crows well.

S.—

Talk of the cruelty of men, what beast that lives has the slow unsparing brutality of a jealous woman? Wanda! Wanda!

SCENE 7TH.

Wanda—

My God! what is it? are the children——

S.—

No! no!! the children are well; it is worse than death! Wanda, I have come so tell you the sin of my life, the shame of it. Oh how will you ever believe that I loved you since I wronged you so.

Wanda—

Tell me! tell me everything! why not have trusted me? Tell me, I am strong.

S.—

Wanda, I am Vassia Kazan, the natural son of the Prince Paul Ivanovich Zabaroff. Up to nine years old I dwelt with my grandmother, a Persian woman on the great plain between the Volga water and the Ural range; thence I was taken to Lycee Clovis, a famous college. Prince Zaberoff I never saw but one day in my Volga village, until when I was fifteen years old I was sent to his house, *Fleur de Roi*, near Villede Ville, where I remained two months. I then returned to the Lycee, and stayed there two years unnoticed by him. One day I was summoned by the principal and told abruptly that the Prince Zaberoff was dead; my protector, as they termed him, and that I was penniless, with the world before me. I could not hope to make you understand tne passions that raged in me, you who have always been in the light of fortune, and always at the head of a mighty family could comprehend nothing of the somber hatred, the futile revolts, the bitter wrath against heaven and humanity, which consumed me then. Thus left alone, without even the remembrance of a word from my father, I should have returned straightway to the Volga plains and buried my feverish griefs under their snows, had not I known that grandmother, Maritza, the only living being I had ever loved, had died half a year after I had been taken from her to be sent to the school in Paris. You see, had I been left there, I should have been a hunter of wild things, or a raftsman on the Volga all my years, and have done no harm. I was a true Russian noble, though a bastard one, and those three months which I had passed at *Fluer de Roi*, had intoxicated me with a thirst for pleasure, and enervated me with a longing to be rich and idle. When Paul Zaberoff died he left me nothing—not even a word. It was true he died suddenly. I quitted the Lycei Clavis with my clothes and my books; I had nothing else in the world. I sold some of these and got to Havre; there I took passage on a barque going to Mexico with wine. The craft was unseaworthy; she went down with all hands off the Pinos Islands, and I, swimming for miles alone, reached the shore. The women were good to me; I got away in a canoe, and

rowed many miles and many days; the sea was calm and
I had bread, fruit and water, enough to last two weeks.
At the end of ten days I neared a brig which took me to
Mexico. My adventurous voyage made me popular there.
I gave a false name of course, for I hated the name of
Vassia Kazan. War was going on at that time with Mexico, and I went and offered my services to the military
adventurer then in command ; bands of Indians fell on us
in great numbers; I was shot down and left for dead; a
stranger found me the morning after, carried me to his hut,
and saved my life by his skill and cure. The stranger
was the Marquis Xavier de Sabran, who had dwelt for
nearly seventy years in the solitude of those vergin forests,
which nothing ever disturbed except the hiss of an Indian's
arrow or the roar of the woods on fire. His influence upon me was the noblest I had ever been subject to; he did
me nothing but good ; his son had died early, having wedded a Spanish Mexican. Ere he was twenty his grandson
had died of snake-bite; he had been of my age; at times
he almost seemed to think this lad lived again in me. I
spent eight years of my life with him ; I saw no European
all those years ; the only men I came in contact with were
Indians and half breeds ; the dense, close-woven forest was
between us and the rest of the world; our only highway
was a river made almost inaccessible by dense fields of
reeds, and banks of jungle, and swamps covered with high
lillies. Eight whole years passed ; so I was twenty five
years old when my protector and friend died of sheer old
age, in one burning summer, against whose burning heat
he had no strength; he talked long and tenderly to me
e'er he died; told me where to find all his papers, and gave
me everything he owned; it was not much. He made me
one last request, that I would collect his manuscripts, complete them and publish them in France. For some weeks
after his death I could think of nothing but his loss. I buried him myself with the aid of an Indian who had loved
him, and his grave is there besides the ruins he so revered,
beneath a grove of cypress; I carved a cross in cedar wood
and raised it above the grave ; I found all his papers where
he had indicated, underneath one of the temple porticoes;
his manuscripts I already had in my possession ; these buried papers were all those which had been brought with
him from France by his Jesuit tutors, and the certificates

of his own and his father's birth and marriage, and those of his son and of his grandson who had died at eighteen years of age. There was also a paper containing directions how to find other documents with the orders and patents of nobility of the Sabrans of Romiris, which had been hidden in the oak wood upon their sea shore in Morbihan; all these he had desired me to seek and take. Now came upon me the temptation to a great sin. The age of his grandson, the young Rene de Sabran, had been mine. It seemed to me that if I assumed his name I should do no one any wrong; to be brief, I was sorely tempted, and I gave way to the temptation. I had no difficulty in claiming recognition in the City of Mexico as the Marquis de Sabran; I was recognized by all the proper authorities, and returned to France as the Marquis de Sabran. On my voyage I made the acquaintance with ten Frenchmen of very high station who proved true friends to me, and had power enough to protect me from the consequences of not having served a military term in France. I saw by French journals that Vassia Kazan had been numbered among the crew who had gone down with the Pinos. On my arrival I first went so Romaris; there I found the papers that were hidden in the oakwood above the sea. The priest and peasants welcomed me with rapture. The Britons never forget; I had no fear of recognition; I had changed so much in my nine years absence that no one could recognize the collegian Vassia Kazan in the Marquis de Sabran. I will not linger on the causes that made me take the name I did; I never did anything that degraded it, as men of the world read degradation; perhaps I should not have satisfied severe moralists, but my one crime apart I was a man of honor until I loved you. I do not attempt to defend my marriage with you; it was a crime, a fraud. I was born a serf in Russia. Now there are no more serfs there; but Alexander who affranchised them cannot affranchise me. I am base born; I cannot ask your forgiveness. Would that God would strike me dead at your feet.

Wanda—

You!—you! You Vassia Kazan!

SCENE 8TH.

V.—
    Does she live ?

G.—
    That is all.

V.—
    Can I see her ?

G.—
    It would be useless; she would not know your Excellency.

S.—
    Allow me the honor of a word with you, Prince : Did you give up my secret to your brother's wife ?

V.—
    Can you ask that? you had my promise.

S.—
    Madam Brancka knows all that you know; she said you had betrayed me to her. She would have told Wanda, I chose sooner to tell her myself; the shock has killed the child, it may kill her! Your sister-in-law is here; if she has used your name falsely, it is for you to avenge it.

V.—
    Tell me what passed between you!

S.—
    Madam Brancka has always been envious of your cousin; when she got possession of the story of my past, she used it without mercy. She would have told my wife with brutality; I told her myself, hoping to spare her something by my own confession. Madam Brancka affirmed to me twice or thrice over that you had given her all the information against me.

V.—
    How could you believe her ? you had my promise.

S.—
    How could I doubt her.

V.—
    You might sooner have doubted anything than that I should have intrusted Countess Brancka with such a secret. How can she have learned your history. Have you betrayed yourself.

S.—

Never since you did not tell her, I cannot conceive how or where she learned it; not a soul lives that knows me as—(Exit Sabran).

V.—

My brother is unfortunate he has wedded a vile wom-an; leave her to me. (Enter Olga).

V.

I hear you have been useing my name falsely to the husband of Wanda;—That you have dared to give me as authority for accusations against him. What is your excuse? What is your excuse-I ask again; Why did you come into this house to injure Wanda Von Szalras? How did you dare to use my name to do her that injury?

O.

I wish to do her a service! Since she has married an adventurer—an imposter—she ought to know it and be free.

V.—

What authority have you for calling the Marquis de Sabran an adventurer; to him you employed my name as your authority. What truth was beneath that lie.

O.—

You know that he is Vassia Kazan.

V.—

Who is Vassia Kazan.

O.—

He is—the man who robbed you of Wanda.

V.—

He could not rob me of what I never possessed; what grounds have you for calling him by that name.

O.—

I have reasons to believe it.

V.—

Reasons to believe it; you told him you heard this this story from myself.

O.—

He never denied it.

V.—

I am not concerned to discuss what he did or did not do; I came here to know on what grounds you employed my name.

O.—

Egon; I will tell you the truth.

V.—

Can you?

O.—

Yes I can and will. I once heard you call him Vassia
Kazan and when I was at Faroc I saw a fragment of a
letter in Sabrans writing on it, I saw the name of Vassia
Kazan. Then I heard something from Russia, I sent
people to Mexico, I had always had my suspicions. I do
not say I have any legal proof but I am morally convinced
that he is no Marquis de Sabran and that he was born a
serf near the city of Kazin; I have changed him with it
and he has as good as confessed. He was struck dumb.

V.—

You saw a fragment of a letter of which you know
nothing. You formed some vague suspicions and because
you have invented a theory of your own you deem you
have a title to ruin the happiness of your cousins home,
and your father you work upon me. Often have I pitied
my brother, but never so deeply as now.

O.—

If my so called discoveries were false, why did he not
say so. If my charges had been baseless would he have
said he would tell his wife himself rather than let her hear
it from me.

V.—

I neither know or care what he said I have only your
version for it you must pardon me if I do not attach Im-
plicit credence to your word. Had you kuown for
certainty such a history you would had you had any
decency or feeling have consulted your husband and myself on the best means of shielding our cousins honor but
you have always envied and hated her; what is her husband to you? But you did a dangerous thing when you
used my name, I will waste no more words upon you you
will sign what I write now or you will repent it.

O.—

My dear Egon what authority have you over me even
if you invest yourself in your brothers, that accounts for
very little I assure you.

O.—

Perhaps so. But if my brother be too careless of his

honor and too credulous of your deceptions he is yet man enough to resent such infamy as you have been guilty of—you will sign this. (Reads) I Olga, Countess Brancka do acknowledge that I most untruthfully used the name of my husbands brother, the prince Vasarhely in an endeavor to injure the gentleman known as the Marquis de Sabran and I do here by ask the pardon of them both and confess that in such pardon I receive great leniency and for bearance. Sign it.

O.—

Pshaw!

V.—

Will you sign it or not; (she tears it). It is easily rewritten. Do not be so foolish Olga. You are a clever woman and always consult your own interests, you will sign at once or you will regret it greatly.

O.—

Why should I sign it; the man is what I say; he could not deny it. If I only guessed at the truth I guessed aright. I wonder that you do not see your interests lie in exposing him. When the world knows he is an impastor, Wanda will divorce him and put the children under other names in religious houses, then you will be able to marry her.

V.—

My cousin will never seek a divorce nor shall I wed with a divorced woman; you sign this paper or I will telegraph for my brother.

O.—

For Stefan my husband.

V.—

Yes Stefan! You may despese him because you can lead him in to mad follies and can make him believe you are an innocent woman but he is not the ignoble dupe you think him he would not bear your infidelity to him if he really knew it nor o her things I know. Two years ago you took two hundred thousand florins worth of diamonds in my name from a jeweler, those I paid for to and did not betray you, and if he knew you had taken money from the young Duc de Blois your richest lover do not think he would be the easily cozened fool you deem him I have only named two, now you sign this or I will tell my brother No! he would not divorce you that is not the way of our family. A religious house or imprisonment in one of hls Siberian places, then good bye to your lovers and your friends you eould cry for them in vain ; now sign.

O.—

No, no, Egon you know well he is what I say he is an impostor. If you were the hero I always thought you, would tear his heart out of his breast ; shoot him like a wolf of his own woods! if her honor is yours; avenge her dishonor.

V.—

You have been told what I shall do if you do not sign this. If you desire to hear any more episodes of your pist, I can tell you many.

O.—

No, no, Egon I implore you do as I ask. Egon I beseech you ! I pray you——.

V.—

You are a good actress.

O.

I am ill ; call my woman.

V.

You are no more ill than I am here woman you sign this now.

O.—

(Signs the paper). You know very well it is true; would she lie dying of it if it were only a lie.

V.—

I know no', your cirrlage is ready now go; if you ever speak of this, remember my silence is only conditional.

O.—

For the first time I have failed. (Exit).

V.—

(Enter *Sabran*).

Here ! You are safe from her. She cannot tell your story to the world. She will not dare even to whisper it as a conjecture. For the first time I have concealed the truth, I affected to disbelieve her story ; there was no other way to save it from publicity. I shall wait here until the danger is past or Wanda is called to God.

S.—

My God is this some hideous nightmare, or have I lost my reason. I have only met my just judgement; if I could only suffer alone, I would not rebel against my doom but to smite her so.

ACT 4.

Scene 1.

Wanda.—
    My cousin—is he here?
Greswold.—
    He is my lady.
W.—
    Bid him come to me. (Enter *Vasaahely*).
Vasarhely.—
    Wanda I am here.
W.—
    Is it true.
V.—
    Yes—.
W.—
    And you knew it.
V.—
    Too late! But Wanda—my beloved Wanda—trust
to me! The world shall never know.
W.—
    The Countess Olga.
V.—
    She is in my power—I will deal with her—she will be
silent as the grave—oh, my injured angel fear not I will
avenge you.
W.—
    No, no, not that; he is my children's father; he
must be sacred. Give me your word, Egon, there shall
be no blood shed between him and you.
V.—
    I am your next friend; you are insulted and dishon-
ored; your race is affronted and stained. Who shall
avenge that, if not your kinsman? there is no male of your
house; it falls to me.
W.—
    Promise me you will not.
V.—
    Your brothers are dead; I may well stand in their
place; then swords would have found him out ere he were
an hour older.

W.—

My brothers are dead, and I forbid anyone to meddle with my life; if anyone slew him it would be I—I— in my own right. I forbid you—I forbid you ; give me your word.

V.—

You are my law; I will do nothing that you forbid. (leaves her.)

W.—

Bloodshed! Bloodshed! Though rivers of blood rolled between him and me, what could wash away the shame that is with me forever? What could death do? Death could blot out nothlng.

W.—

Greswold, leave me and ask my husband to come here.

G.—

My lady—

W.—

Be as good as to go to my husband at once. (Exit *Greswold.*)

(Enter *Sabran.*) I have but little to say to you, but that little is best said and not written. Af·er that which you have told me, you must know my life cannot be lived out beside yours. The law gives you many rights, no doubt, but I believe you will not be so base as as to enforce them.

S.—

I have no rights; I am a criminal before the law. The law will free you from me if you choose.

W.—

I do not so choose; you understand me ill. I do not carry my wrongs or woes to others. What you have told me is known only to Prince Vasaihely and to the Countess Brancka. He will be silent and has the power to make her so. The world need know nothing. Can you think that I shall be its informant?

S.—

If you divorce me—

W.—

What could divorce do for me? Could it de·stroy the past? Neither church nor law can undo what you have done. Divorce would make me feel that in the past I had been your mistress, not your wife. Neither priest nor judge can efface the past. No power, human or divine, can free me purify me. Wash your dishonored blood from your children's veins. I shall not seek for a legal separation; that is, if you do not force me to do so to protect myself from you. I wish no words between us; you know your sin; all your life has been a lie. I will keep me and mine back from vengeance, but do not mistake. God may forgive you; I never! What I desire to say to you is that henceforth you will give up the name you stole; you shall be known only as you have been here of late—as the Count von Idrae. The title was mine to give; I gave it to you. No wrong is done, save to my fathers, who were brave men.

S.—

The children—

W.—

They are mine. You will not I believe, seek to enforce your title to dispute them with me.

S.—

Once you said that repentence washes out all crimes. Will you count my remorse as nothing?

W.—

You would have known no remorse had your secret never been discovered.

S.—

That is not true, but how can I hope you will believe me? And once you told me there was no sin you would not pardon me.

W.—

We pardon sin; we do not pardon baseness. You will leave Hohenszalres; you will go where you will; you have the revenues of Idrac if they be insufficient to support you.

S.—

Do you insult me—so

W.—

Insult you!! You must live as becames the rank due to my husband. The world need suspect nothing; it will only believe that we are tired of each other, like so many. The blame will be placed on me. You are a brilliant comedian and can humor and please the world. You will meet my abstainence by the only amends you can make to me! Let me forget—as far as I am able—let me forget that ever you lived. You have heard me! now, go!

S.—

But you loved me; you loved me so well.

W.—

Do not recall that. Women of my race have killed men before now for less outrage than yours has been to me.

S.—

Kill me! I will kiss your hand. Believe, at least, that I loved you; believe that, at least.

W.—

Sir, I have been your dupe for ten long years. I can be so no more.

SCENE 2.

Gela.—

Do you know I think our mother is changing to marble she, will soon be of stone like the statues in the chapel. When I touch her I feel cold.

Bela.—

You are ungrateful, you little child. Who loves who cares for us; who thinks of us as our mother does? If her lips are cold perhaps her heart is broken. We are only children; we know so little.

Gela.—

But will he never come back; shall we never see him again; perhaps he is dead.

Bela.—

How dare you say that Gela; if he were—were—that we should be told it; oh, no! he is not dead there would be masses in the chapel, he would send down some angel to tell us.

Gela.—

Why do you care so much for him? It must be him he who made our mother so unhappy, it is her we should most love. You say he told you so.

Bela.—

I think he would not wish us to talk of it we will pray for him that is all we can do. (Exit Gela).

Gela.—

If it should be? If it should be? (Enter Wanda).

Wanda.—

What is it Bela, you ought not to come here.

Bela.—

May I ask you just one thing?

Wanda.—

Surely my child are you afraid ot me.

Bela.—

Gela said he might be dead.   Oh, if he ever dies will you please tell me.

Wanda.—

I have forbidden you to speak of your father, if it be he you mean.

Bela.—

But he may die.   Will you tell me; please will you tell me?   I will never ask anything else—never—never.

Wanda.—

Why do you cling on to his memory.   He never took heed of you.

Bela.—

I was so little.   But I loved him.   Oh I loved him, and I was the last to see him that night.

Wanda.—

I know—!   You are right to feel so.   Cherish his memory and pray for him always; but do not speak of him to me.   When you are grown to manhood, if I be living then, you shall hear what parted your father and me. You shall judge us yourself.   But there are many years to that many weary years to me.   I shall endeavor that they be happy ones for you; but you must never ask me, never speak of him.   I gave you that command once before, but you are very young, you have forgotten.

Bela.—

I had not forgotten.   But if what Gela said should ever be, will you tell me.   I will never disobey again, but pray—pray—tell me.

Wanda.—

I will tell you—if I know, but fear not he will out live me; now my dear leave me I am occupied.   (Enter Princess Ottilie.

Princess O.—

Wanda! Wanda you are a Christian woman it is Christian never to forgive.

W.—

What is forgiveness.   It is abstainence from vengeance?   I have abstained.

O.—
It is far more than that.

W. —
Then I do not reach it.

O.—
No you do not; is it in consonence with your tenets, with your duties?

W.—
I think so.

O.—
Then my dear change your creed.

W.—
I have the blood in me of men who were not always Christians, but who even when Pagan Knew what honor was; there are some things which are so vile that one must be vile oneself before one can forgive them.

O.—
I am in ignorance of the nature of your wrong but this I know. They erred who gave you absolution at eastertide while you still bore bitterness in your soul.

W.—
Would I lay bare my soul and his shame to any priest. Dear aunt believe me I have been more merciful than many would have been.

O.—
You mean that you have not sought for a divorce, nay, that is not mercy. That is decency, dignity, self-respect. That you have done is not mercy. Wanda you were so happy, he was so devoted. Can all that have crumbled like a house of sand.

W.—
What did I say once, the day of my betrothal! that I leaned on a reed. The reed has withered; that is all; as for forgiveness, what is the obligation of forgiveness. It is the obligation to pardon infidelity, unkindness, cruelty but not dishonor, to forgive dishonor is to be dishonored, so would my father have said.

Scene 3.

Wanda.—
I was harsh to you yesterday my child. I came to tell you that you were quite right to have the thought you had. You are his son you must not forget him.

Bela.—

I am glad I may remember, when I am a man I will go and find him and bring him back. She is very unhappy; if I could find him now perhaps it would make her happy. (Enter Otto).

Otto.—

My little lord. I have something to tell you.

Bela.—

Of him?

Otto.—

My lord; your father has been seen on the other side of the Glockner by my underling Fritz. I made bold to tell you Count Bela, for I had given you my word.

Bela.---

I knew if he had died I should have known it. Tell me more; tell me more, quick.

Otto.----

There is no more to tell my little lord. Fritz will swear that he saw your father. Though there were many fathoms of ice and snow between them, he says there was no mistaking the way he sighted his rifle and fired.

Bela.---

Then he lives and I can find him.

Otto.----

Yes, he lives; the lord be praised.

Bela.---

I will go and bring him back and then she will smile again.

Scene.

Bela.----

I wish Gela had come, but it would have been no use to ask him he will never disobey even to make good come, of it I am so tired and lame; but then if it did not hurt it would be nothing to do. What is that? An eagle! Oh you great bird, you are treacherous, you are thankless, we have spared you and yours always and now you will kill me. Do you not hear? Do you not hear? I do not fear you, you great bird come take me if you will and can. If I could only take him home--·once--I would not mind dying here afterwards but with that undone it is cruel. (A

shot is heard and Sabran appears). Oh my father----my
father - -I came to find you.—
Sabran. ---

Oh tell me where your mother kissed you last, that I
may set my lips there. My God he is freezing. There is
but one way to get him to the hut that is leap the chasm
there, around it would be miles ; he would die e'r I reached it, Ah my poor child the snow is in my blood and my
blood is yours and now it claims us. No I must not sleep,
this fatal desire to lie down and rest is but the frost that
kills. God grant me power to save him for his mother's
sake. There is but one way to escape---to leap the fissure.—
God help me! (He leaps).

SCENE 4.

Bela.-- -

Is that you?
Sabran.—

It is I, my child if you can move, try and creep to the
hut and call; I cannot. He is brave, he has his mother's
courage.
Bela.—

(At the hut). It is I, Count Bela; come to my father
quick (the jigers, rush out and find Sabran). You cannot
move fa her.
Sabran.—

I am stiff from the cold ; nothing more (to the men).
One of you if it be possible, go to the burg. Tell the
Countess von Szalras that her son is safe. You need not
speak of me. Bring the physician here when it is morning but say nothing of me to night. Give me a little of
your wine—for I think I am hurt unto death.
Bela.—

You are hurt; you are hurt; and all for me!
Sabran.--

My child do not grieve so ; it is nothing; a mere
momentary wrench, do not even think of it, I am not in
pain. Warm some wine and give it to my son, then wrap
him up warmly and make him sleep before the fire.
Bela.—

You are hurt, you are ill. I came to find you and
take you back. Our mother has never been the same—
she has never smiled———

Sabran.—

Hush! Do not speak of your mother before these men, her servants. You came to seek me, my poor little boy? That was good of you and it was good to remember me.

Beln.—

The others have always prayed for you, because they were told. But me, I have loved you always; I have never thought of anything else, and I have tried to be so good. Oh! I have tried.

Sabran.—

(*aside*) (When I am dead, and I shall be so soon, will he remember, too?) My child, it is very sweet to me to hear your voice again. But if you love me, now obey me. Allow yourself to be undressed, drink some warm wine and lie down before the fire. Do not be afraid, you will see me when you are awake. I shall not stir, (*aside*) No, I shall never stir again. They will bear me away to my grave, that is all. I am like a felled tree. All is over. Well, perchance so best. When I am dead, she may forgive, she may love the children. (to the jagers) Now the child sleeps. Get my clothes off me, if you can. Touch me gently; I think my back is broken.

SCENE 5.

Wanda.—

Does fate chastise me for my own cruelty. I have exiled them from me because their sweet faces were like his. Does God punish me through them, Oh my Bela, my darling, my first born. Yes, you are his, but, more than all, you are mine!

Gela.—

Mother, I dare not say it before, but now I must. I think—I think—Bela is gone to try and bring him home.

W.—

Him! You mean—your father.

G.—

Yes.

W.—

What makes you think so?

G.—

He was always talking of it. Yesterday, he was so strange, and when we went to bed he kissed me a great many times, and he prayed a long, long time. He would have taken his sword for nothing else I think. I—I heard the men say to-day that our father was somewhere near, and I think that Bela might have heard it and gone to find him.

W.—

Will he rob me even of my first born?

(*Enter Greswold.*)

You have found my Bela.

Gres.—

Yes, your brother is quite safe! My lady hears.

W.—

Bring him! bring him at once!—oh! my child. Who found him? If a peasant saved his life, he and his shall have the finest of my land in Iselthal in grant forever and forever.

Gres.—

May I speak to your Excellency alone?

W.—

Go, my darling and bear the good news to your grand-aunt. You know how she has suffered. (*Exit Gela.*) Now, tell me all.

Gres.—

My lady, his father found your son.

W.—

His father! How came he there?

G.—

My lady, your husband has dwelt among the Glock-ner slopes since he went away. Few knew it. The few kept the secret. I was one of them—

W.—

Go on, he found my child, you say.

G.—

He found Count Bela! Yes, he knew nothing of Count Bela's loss, but he saw a young boy threatened by an eagle and shot the bird. The keeper said that my lord desired you should hear of the safety of the child, but not of his own presence in the hut; but I thought your Excellency should be told of all.

W.—

You were right; I thank you. You have been ever faithful to me and mine. (*Exit Greswold.*) Oh, my love!

64

my love! We will live our lives out together. (Enter
Princess Ottillie.)
O.—

Is it true? Is the child found?
W.

Yes! his father has found him. Dear mother, you
have long condemned me, judged me unchristian, unmer-
ciful, harsh. I know not whether you were right or I, God
knows; we cannot. But give me your blessing ere I go
out into the night. I go to him. I will bring him here.
O.—

Bring him? Your child?
W.—

My husband.
O.—

Heaven will be with you.
W.—

Who can tell! perhaps my harshness will make heaven
harsh to me. Bid them saddle a horse, used to the hills
and let Otto and two other men be ready to go with me.

SCENE 6.

Wanda.—
I have come to thank you.
S.—

Ah, for the childs sake; you do not come for me.
W.—

I came for you. I will forget all else save, I once
loved you.
S.—

It cannot be, it cannot be!
W.—

You were my lover; you are my children's father. You
shall return to us. Your sin was great, yes but love
pardons all sins, nay effaces them, makes them as if they
were not; I know that now, what have not been my own
sins, my coldness my cruel unyielding pride. Nay sometimes, I have thought of late my fault was darker than
your own, more hateful in God's sight.
S.—

Noblest of all women always, if it be true—yes it be
true—stoop down and kiss me once again. (Kisses him.)
I am happy, I have lived among your hills almost ever

since that night, that I might see vour shadow as you pass-
ed ; hear the feet of your horses in the woods. The men
were faithful they never told. Kiss me once more, you
believe, say you believe now that I did love you though
I wronged you so.
W.—
   I do believe, I think God cannot pardon me that I
ever doubted. Sabran ! Sabran! Oh my love, are you
hurt? speak, speak, cannot you move? Look at me !
Speak to me !
S.—
   Nay, love, I shall not move again, my spine is hurt—
Not broken, I believe, but hurt beyend help. Paralysis
has begun. My angel, grieve not for me, I shall die
happy. You love me still Ah, it is best thus! Were
I to live, my sin, my shame, might still torture you, still part
us, but when I am dead you will forget them, you are so
generous you will forget them ; you will only remember
that we were happy once, happy through many a long
sweet year, and that I loved you,—loved you in all truth I
though I betrayed you.